STEP INTO READING® will help your child get there. The program offers five steps to reading success. Each step includes fun stories and colorful art or photographs. In addition to original fiction and books with favorite characters, there are Step into Reading Non-Fiction Readers, Phonics Readers and Boxed Sets, Sticker Readers, and Comic Readers—a complete literacy program with something to interest every child.

Learning to Read, Step by Step!

Ready to Read   Preschool–Kindergarten
• big type and easy words • rhyme and rhythm • picture clues
For children who know the alphabet and are eager to begin reading.

Reading with Help   Preschool–Grade 1
• basic vocabulary • short sentences • simple stories
For children who recognize familiar words and sound out new words with help.

Reading on Your Own   Grades 1–3
• engaging characters • easy-to-follow plots • popular topics
For children who are ready to read on their own.

Reading Paragraphs   Grades 2–3
• challenging vocabulary • short paragraphs • exciting stories
For newly independent readers who read simple sentences with confidence.

Ready for Chapters   Grades 2–4
• chapters • longer paragraphs • full-color art
For children who want to take the plunge into chapter books but still like colorful pictures.

STEP INTO READING® is designed to give every child a successful reading experience. The grade levels are only guides; children will progress through the steps at their own speed, developing confidence in their reading. The F&P Text Level on the back cover serves as another tool to help you choose the right book for your child.

Remember, a lifetime love of reading

For Gina

Little Critter® Goes To School book, characters, text, and images © 2020 Mercer Mayer
Little Critter, Mercer Mayer's Little Critter, and Mercer Mayer's Little Critter and Logo are
registered trademarks of Orchard House Licensing Company.

All rights reserved. Published in the United States by Random House Children's Books, a division
of Penguin Random House LLC, 1745 Broadway, New York, NY 10019, and in Canada by Penguin
Random House Canada Limited, Toronto. Originally published in a different form as *Little
Critter's This Is My School* by Golden Books, New York, in 1990.

Step into Reading, Random House, and the Random House colophon are registered trademarks of
Penguin Random House LLC.

Visit us on the Web!
StepIntoReading.com
rhcbooks.com
littlecritter.com

Educators and librarians, for a variety of teaching tools, visit us at RHTeachersLibrarians.com

ISBN 978-1-9848-3097-5 (trade) — ISBN 978-1-9848-5099-7 (lib. bdg.) —
ISBN 978-1-9848-3098-2 (ebook)

Printed in the United States of America

10 9 8 7 6 5 4 3 2

LITTLE CRITTER® GOES TO SCHOOL

by Mercer Mayer

Random House New York

Today is my
first day of school.

I have new things
to wear.

I have a new pencil
and a notebook.

Mom gives me
money for lunch.

Mom gives me an
apple for the teacher.

I want to
give the teacher
my new bug.

Mom says an apple
is better.

Mom waits with me
for the school bus.
She does not have to wait,
because I am big.

But it makes her happy.

The bus is full.

The driver is quiet.

We are not.

We are having fun.

12

I know where to go.
But I ask someone
anyway.

My teacher is Miss Kitty.

I give her my apple.

We have a lot of things!

We put them away.

Miss Kitty gives us name tags.

I sit at my desk.

There are many kids

I do not know.

We talk about
our summer vacations.
My family went camping.
A bear took our food.

We learn a song.

Some kids do not sing.

We draw pictures.
I draw my family.

Then we play outside.

After playtime,

Miss Kitty reads a story.

The bell rings.

It is time for lunch.

I buy lunch

all by myself.

I sit with some
other kids.
We trade food.

After lunch,
we have rest time.
I am not tired.

But I have to
lie down anyway.

After rest time,
we go to the library.

There are so many
books here!

Then it is time
to go home.

Miss Kitty helps us
onto the bus.

Tomorrow is
show-and-tell.
I think I will bring
my pet snake.